THE ELEMENTS

MAHEEN F.

Contents

THE FIRST ELEMENT

THE SECOND ELEMENT

THE MEET UP OF WATER AND ICE

SEARCHING FOR WIND ELEMENT

NEWS PAPER IN KOREA

THE FOURTH ELEMENT

THE GOAL

THE MAGICAL WOODS

THE MAGICAL WOOD 2

THE CAVE

THE DRAGON

TEAM UNKNOWN

THE CONSTITUTION BOOK OF ELEMENT

RULES OF BOOK

GEM STORY

New Journey 31

THE FIRST ELEMENT

This story begains with a girl named Alice, she has the power of ice and couldn't control it, she think people will kill her,thinking that she is a alien because she live in the most warm place in the US.But her parents fully support her. When she turn 20 she stay at a hotel which is in Alaska ,the coldest place in the U.S . She was bored so she read a book and that book was about"**the elements**" she found the answer that a non fictional book can never answer and she found out she is one of the element, but now she was tired so to give herself a break she, start watching televsion.

Alice was just skipping channels but one of them stops her break.

THE SECOND ELEMENT

Yes, that channel was from Dubai,it was very popular,the channel was named after a girl named Lisa, and it was all about her.People think she was some kind of magician but trust me she was a lot more than that.

She was the second element,the water element, she make water dance with her finger. And unlike Alice she was very comfortable with her powers but didn't reveal she has powers ,and she just let people make rumors about her. And Lisa thought she was the only one with powers.

THE MEET UP OF WATER AND ICE

As Lisa was popular, Alice did some research on Lisa and somehow found her address,Alice have enough money to travel to Dubai,after 14 hours she found Lisa's house, but it was surrounded by bodyguards, so this is the first time Alice is going to use her power, to make stairs to Lisa's room from her window and she did it perfectly.

Lisa was not in her room, so Alice was waiting sitting on lisa's couch " after half pass hour " Lisa came in and was speechless and she was about to call the security but then Alice said this" i know you have the power of water but you're not alone there are other elements like us too" Lisa was like " there's no way this is possbile" but then Alice told her the whole story and show her outside her window ,and it all make sense.

SEARCHING FOR WIND ELEMENT

Lisa and Alice were confused who can be the third element,but then something comes to Lisa's mind she remembered that there was a guy in her school who was Lisa's friend, he was kinda nerd but also the topper of the whole school. His name was Drake. But somehow he can control wind and play with wind. Alice said " can you contact him" lisa take her phone out and search and found him. Lisa said "but i have no idea that he still use this number" she call him , it was ringing but nobody was answering and finally someone pick it up.

NEWS PAPER IN KOREA

HELLO , HELLO ? Drake said. It was a relief for Lisa and Alice , and now Lisa said " answer me this question where did you live", Drake said " ok i dont live in Dubai anymore I live in Korea and *gives address* " Alice said i dont have enough money to travel to Korea. Lisa was like wait i am your friend and rich just ask it . They both went to Korea on his address and found Drake .Lisa to Alice " wow Drake changed so much" .Lisa ask you can control wind , huh ? Drake seem nervous and said " why ,that is fictional ", Lisa said " stop lying i know" ,then drake thought he should tell the truth so he did but he was shock that weren't surprise then he get to know that they are like him and Lisa tell him the story. then after all this ,Alice said i am exhausted and want a break can we just not talk about this for only a day . Lisa and Drake totally understand . Alice love reading so she found a newspaper and start reading it , she read the first page of the newspaper and was shock to read it . Two days ago a little child was surrounded by wild fire and a boy went through the fire without getting a single burn and save the little child .

THE FOURTH ELEMENT

And now that guy is famous, Alice found this news and thought that this would end her break again , so she didn't tell this to Lisa . while Alice finish reading her news paper , Drake and Lisa were totally stressed out about the fourth element , Alice came from another room ,Lisa "do you have any idea for the fourth element" , Alice said " no idea" , then Lisa replied " have you read the newspaper its seem like you fully read it", alice " ahh yess" Lisa" ok lets see what can we find in the newspaper",Lisa went to grab it from the room but Alice immediantely stop her but Lisa didn't stop and went to grab it , Alice take the newspaper in the hand and won't give it to lisa , lisa" what's wong with you " and Lisa snatched it but luckily Alice tear the first page.

Lisa noticed it and said" give me this paper , now !" Alice finally give up and give it , Lisa read it and said " ahhhhhh, why do you do this Alice, i know you dont want your break to end but, aghh but fighting is not the solution so , maybe we know who is the fourth element but how can we found him .

Drake gently, take the newspaper from Lisa and said we can meet him tomorrow because tomorrow is his live interview in Downtown (a place in Korea) . The next day they went to downtown and found him , after his interview Lisa ask him can she have a second and Lisa was already a star and the boy was his fan and the first thing he said was " hi I am your biggest fan and my name is kim joug wan but you can call me Sam" Lisa " now tell me the truth you can control fire right? ", without hesitation Sam tell Lisa the truth and Lisa tell him the whole story

THE GOAL

Lisa to Sam " you know me and now you know the other elements
" then Drake and Alice showed up and they greet each other ,while
a question pops up in Alice's mind she said " are there only four
elements of us or there are more left ? , Lisa replied " no idea dude I
think its only four of us and lets focus on our goal but wait, what's
our goal ? " Drake " why are we choosed to be the elements ? Sam "
I can't believe I am working with you guys * everyone face plams*

And suddenly a cat broke into Drake's house and comes to Alice
and give her a letter which was from a team name **team unknown**
it says " dear elements you have done a great job, searching for the
elements, hats off to you guys , now lets come to the point you
have hard job , you need to go to the fanasty woods which is a little
bit dangerous so get some supplies there and there's a cave full of
gems and crystals you need to go inside and find
the**CONSTITUTION BOOK OF ELEMENTS*** and you maybe
need us in the future, constitution will tell you the goal and why
were you guys choosen , now thank you and bye.* it also attached
some rings to teleport there.

THE MAGICAL WOODS

Alice said "this is amazing guys we will gather stuff like swords,shields, clothes , sleeping bags,food and medicines and gather resources we are going tomorrow " Lisa " yes, guys we need to be pack our stuff today ,have important things to keep us safe and yea drake it's your duty to bring a lighter for born fire ", drake " sure and you sam bring food and medicines, sam " so are you guys ready for tomorrow " , everyone " yessssssssssss! " the next day they bravely enter the woods , they were wearing shields and were ready , Alice "wow ! this is so beautiful, Sam was shock and was going to faint , drake " can we leave this drama king here " , Lisa told him he might help us to continue their journey , after 3 hours of walking they were fed up and don't want to walk , Drake just took a deep breath and exhale it , suddenly all four of them start floating and was still going to there destination . when they were floating in the air drake said " i can't do this anymore i am tired and you guys just have to walk now " they understand and continue to walk but now they need to cross a river it seems to be easy but it has hungry filled with corcodile.

THE MAGICAL WOOD 2

Lisa use her power by lifting the water up with the crorcodiles ,
they cross the river and then the night time comes they set a
bonfire and the final step was to light up the fire but lighter wasn't
working and they were worried but sam save their night by
lightning up the fire. And Alice was leading the group because she
dosen't know how to control her powers, Lisa , Drake and Sam
were forcing her to use them but she don't want to make a mess,
and was even hard for Alice to lead the group and dont know how
to use her powers.

THE CAVE

After 5 days they finally find the cave it was full with purple crystals , they were so happy and they take a deep breath and went in the cave , it was beautiful and after discovering the cave they realize , the cave was vibrating but they just ignore it, and find the **CONSTITUTION BOOK OF ELEMENTS** Alice was about to pick it but she was shaking , *Lisa pat her and said* " you can do it bestie " and Drake and Sam start cherring up Alice and Alice was encouraged enough to pick it up she finally pick it up.

THE DRAGON

But someone **loudly** roar and Alice got scared and drop the book , **IT WAS A ROAR OF A DRAGON** ,and guess what? dragon don't like to be disturbed when they are sleeping but the loud cherring noise make him wake up and he was the body guard of the **constituion book of elements ,** so he was very furious . and those big step of dragons's feet were coming towards there team. And all of them were shaking . Now they find a good hiding spot but all of them were ready to start a fight except Alice , but all of them were forcing Alice but she wasn't ready so only 3 of them were going to fight the dragon but nothing was working because sam was increasing the level of fire, Lisa can't help because the level of fire was so much higher than the level of water and she was just putting out the fire which was burning the cave, and Drake had no idea what to do .Only Alice can freeze dragon's mouth but Alice refuse that and continue to hide , in the end they give up and dragon find their hiding spot, he was going to kill them but in the end ,Alice accept and try to use her power and **it worked out !** she froze his mouth and they were so happy that they survived.

TEAM UNKNOWN

Then 4 people appear and said " you have done a great job" alice said " who are you" and one of the girl who was also the leader of the group said " we are team unknown and we send you the letter i didn't expect that but you guys are brave and we also want to know what's written in the CONSTITUTION BOOK OF ELEMENTS. and we have the same power i am ember and i have the power of ice , she is stain and she has the power of water, he is jordan and he has the power of wind and he is fire ball he has the power of fire they greet eachother.

and then Drake said is it raining in the cave ? *all of them look up* the ice on dragon's mouth is melting so alice froze it again and was going to pick up the book but dragon can see that but and he somehow break the ice and he use a power name anti sheild and using that power, no power can work on him and those eight dosen't know that they were using there power for no reason , Drake realise that what was going on , he ran out of the cave bring a sword and told sam to heat it By using his power, and when dragon was going to use his deadliest move and kill everyone Drake stab the dragon from the back and kill him, that make everyone so happy .

THE CONSTITUTION BOOK OF ELEMENT

Finally Alice pick up the book but it wasn't opening and it dosen't even have a lock just have a empty space to place something on the book cover and ember said " are you guys ready" and team unknown said " yes" and each four of them teleport a gem and give it to Alice .

Alice place them and book was ready but, fire ball stop her and said " i know you guys are tired let's get teleported to Drake's house and then read the book , and after 20 mins they get teleported. and Alice was about to open the book and Alice said "are you ready" everyone said , " yessssss" and she begain to read out loud .

RULES OF BOOK

And the book tell the rules and everything which they already know but it also have story and that story was " that, years ago the one who invent these elements was known as Max and write everything in the **CONSTITUION BOOK OF ELEMENTS**,he didn't even have the idea to give these powers to people but one day Max was fighting with the devil and the devil almost kill Max. Max didn't die but fainted and at that time the devil steal the book , when Max realise that the book was steal by the devil , he gave differnt people the same power and if they didn't get what they have to do Max take it back. The devil died but his pet dragon was the body gaurd of the book.

But 6 people have done the great job and their name are Ember,Fire ball,Stain,Jordan ,Alice,Lisa ,Drake and Sam and now Max think he has done a great job giving power to these people" after reading this,Sam asked we are just reading this **CONTITUTION BOOK OF ELEMENTS** right after as we came across it. So how are name is in the book Fire ball replied " that's the magic" .

GEM STORY

Alice asked " why your team name is in the book what did you guys do" and then Stain said, " we have seen that forest before the find the gems, remember we gave you the gems to insert in the book it took us days to find those but we couldn't defeat the dragons, but we knew next one can defeat the dragon but we still have the gems so when we knew you guys almost defeat the dragon we appear to give you guys gems " , Lisa asked " where did you get those gems then jordan said " we search from cave to cave to find these gems "

*then Alice notice that the book was being written on its own

Book said that if someone did their job perfectly the book will disappear and their power will be taken back from them.

New Journey

and after one hour they noticed that the book disappear and all them understand that it's time they hugged each other and say goodbye to their powers , and suddenly the light of the house went off and the spot light was coming on all eight of them and all of them begain to fly and their power, was gone and the light of the house come back and that time they say bye to each other and booked their flight where they belong to and Lisa payed for Alice , and Alice was finally gonna meet her parents again because this time , she was not going to Alaska now , she was going back to parents . And next day they say a final goodbye and left for their house, except Drake because he was already in his house, and when Alice saw her parents and her parents were happy and proud to know her story and her life was back to normal and it was her first time expreriencing normal life and all of them started a new journey .